12 07/03

THE
HORRIBLY
HAUNTED
SCHOOL

MARGARET MAHY

THE HORRIBLY HAUNTED SCHOOL

Illustrated by Robert Staermose

VIKING

VIKING

Published by the Penguin Group
Penguin Putnam Inc., 375 Hudson Street, New York, New York 10014, U.S.A
Penguin Books Ltd, 27 Wrights Lane, London W8 5TZ, England
Penguin Books Australia Ltd, Ringwood, Victoria, Australia
Penguin Books Canada Ltd, 10 Alcorn Avenue, Toronto, Ontario, Canada, M4V 3B2
Penguin Books (NZ) Ltd, 182-190 Wairau Road, Auckland 10, New Zealand

Penguin Books Ltd, Registered Offices: Harmondsworth, Middlesex, England

First published in Great Britain by Hamish Hamilton Ltd, 1997
First published in the U.S.A. by Viking, a member of Penguin Putnam Inc., 1998

1 3 5 7 9 10 8 6 4 2

Text copyright © Margaret Mahy, 1997
Illustrations copyright © Robert Staermose, 1997

A Vanessa Hamilton Book

Library of Congress Catalog
Card Number: 97-61338

ISBN 0-670-87490-6

Printed in Great Britain by Butler and Tanner Limited
Set in Ehrhardt

Contents

Chapter 1

An Ordinary Boring Day

'Time to go home for breakfast,' Monty Merryandrew said to his friend, Lulu. 'I'm hungry.'

'I'm never hungry,' said Lulu.

'You're lucky,' said Monty. 'Never having to go home for breakfast, 1 mean.'

'I miss the *idea* of breakfast, though,' said Lulu. 'I loved eating when I was alive. What are you going to do *after* breakfast?'

'Go to school,' said Monty gloomily. 'It's just an ordinary, boring day – apart from Mum's jigsaw puzzle championship, that is. I hope she wins this year. She tries hard, and we could do with the money.'

'Well, you will come and play spaceships again

1

after school, won't you?' begged Lulu. 'It's so
boring haunting a car that's never going to be
driven ever again.'

'Of course I will,' Monty promised her. 'See
you later.'

Then he scrambled off through the gorse and
grass, looking forward to his breakfast, and even to
the boring day stretching ahead of him. After all,
he was better off than poor Lulu.

People don't realize how dull it is being a ghost,
he thought. I like that old car, but I wouldn't want

to *haunt* it for fifty years. And what happens after the car has rusted away to nothing? Will Lulu just vanish, or will she have to go on haunting the space where the car used to be?

Monty and Lulu could never make up their minds about this important question. Ghosts are just as mysterious to themselves as they are to anyone else.

All the same, thought Monty, as he edged around the last gorse bush, Lulu is lucky in some ways. She doesn't have to worry about her parents the way I have to worry about mine.

He pushed his way out of the gorse bushes and on to the lawn . . . or what counted as a lawn in the Merryandrew backyard. The grass grew as high as his knees, for Monty's parents were always too busy to cut it. And on that particular morning they were not only busy – they were bothered as well.

Busy and Bothered at Breakfast

Monty bounced into the dining room to find his mother and father sitting cross-legged on the floor, eating breakfast. There was nowhere else to sit because the table was entirely taken up with pieces of a huge jigsaw puzzle. Monty's mother and father scarcely noticed their son, for they were both busy bothering, though about totally different things.

Monty's father was worrying about cars. Only yesterday, the engine of his car – a new second-hand car, bought the week before from a reputable dealer – had stopped at a traffic light. Sparks had sprayed out in a way that was fine for a firework, but most upsetting in a new second-hand car. A whole lot of car experts had rushed over and had quickly decided that the car just wasn't worth repairing. 'It's a total write-off! Don't even try to fix it or you'll be throwing good money after bad,' they said in chorus. Mr Merryandrew, who worked as a government philosopher and knew very little about cars, was overwhelmed with

gloom. He desperately needed a second-hand car dealer whose judgement he could trust.

As for Monty's mother, though she sympathized with her darling husband, *her* thoughts (like the family table) were entirely taken up with jigsaw puzzles.

If I were to win the National Jigsaw Puzzle Championship we would be able to waltz out, laughing and singing, and buy a brand new car, she was thinking to herself. She knew she had a good chance of winning. Her nimble fingers could twinkle any five-hundred-piece puzzle together at the rate of a hundred pieces a minute (which is one and four-tenths of a piece every second), even if it had big stretches of cloudless sky in it. (Doing a big stretch of cloudless sky is one of the great tests for a jigsaw puzzle expert.) But, no matter how well Mrs Merryandrew did with cloudless sky, she always lost points in the free-form section of the championship in which contestants had to invent an entirely new sort of puzzle, and then put it together correctly.

Yet, she was a loving mother. As Monty bounced through the doorway, she gave up her dreams of jigsaw puzzle glory, smiled, and asked him what he had been doing in the garden so early in the morning.

'Playing spaceships with Lulu,' Monty said, for he was an honest boy. 'Lulu loves the idea of visiting other planets, but there were no such things as spaceships when she was actually alive.'

'What do you mean . . . when she was alive?' cried Mrs Merryandrew, her smile quickly giving way to a look of motherly suspicion.

'Mum, I've *told* you about Lulu,' said Monty. 'She's a ghost. She's been haunting that old, rusty car in the corner of the garden for round about seventy years, but she can't hide from me because I'm allergic to ghosts. I begin sneezing whenever there are any unseen ghosts hovering around. As long as they are invisible I sneeze and sneeze, until, at last, they are forced to appear. Either that, or they rush off and do their haunting somewhere else.'

'You silly boy, there are no such things as ghosts. It's *gorse* you are allergic to,' declared Mrs Merryandrew.

'No, it's *ghosts*,' Monty explained patiently. 'Invisible ones. I sneezed and sneezed until Lulu couldn't bear it any longer. She just *had* to show herself. And once a ghost shows itself, my sneezing stops, and we can begin talking. I'm the one doing the sneezing, so I should know.'

Chapter 3

Mrs Merryandrew is Deeply Disturbed

'I am deeply disturbed,' cried Mrs Merryandrew, 'and on the very morning of the championship, too. Now, don't misunderstand me, Monty. I don't mind you being slightly strange, for we have lots of strange people in our family, including your dear grandfather who is studying pretzels in South America . . .'

'Quetzals, Mum, quetzals! A sort of bird!' Monty corrected her, sitting down on the floor between his parents and reaching for the muesli.

'Quetzals-pretzels!' exclaimed his mother. 'I knew it was something in that part of the alphabet. The point is that even your grandfather is not as odd as you, my darling, only son. Here you are, declaring that invisible ghosts make you sneeze, whereas every sensible person knows for *sure* that there are no such things as ghosts, invisible or otherwise. Oh dear, I'm beginning to worry so much that I'll never ever be able to think of anything original for the free-form section of the National Jigsaw Puzzle Championship. And, Monty, if I fail the free-form section, I'll never win the prize, and all this eating off the floor will have been for nothing.' Turning to her husband, she cried, 'Won't you speak to him, my dear?'

Mr Merryandrew sighed deeply, but he wasn't sighing over Monty.

'Who can I trust?' he mumbled. 'When I bought that car, the notice on its windscreen said in large, clear print that it was in immaculate condition. It said it in capital letters. IMMACULATE CONDITION! AMAZING VALUE! That's what it said. Not one mention of possible explosions. Now, if a man can't trust capital letters, what can he trust?'

But as he said this, Mrs Merryandrew was growing impatient. Turning her deep blue gaze on Monty once more, she said, 'Darling boy, I don't mind you playing spaceships in the old car. The future is with science, and I think you'd enjoy outer space. (I'd be so proud and happy to see a child of mine in orbit around Mars.) But I don't

want you believing in ghosts called Lulu. I have made up my mind in one and two-fifths of a second. You must change schools immediately.'

'Change schools!' cried Monty, astonished.

'A new school,' his mother repeated. 'And I know your father agrees with me, though he's deeply distracted at the moment, poor dear. You must be enrolled, without a moment's delay, at the Brinsley Codd School for Sensible Thought.' She nudged Mr Merryandrew. '*You* tell him, dear!'

'Do they teach car repair at the Brinsley Codd School?' asked Mr Merryandrew. 'Could Monty do a crash course?'

'A crash course?' cried Mrs Merryandrew, shuddering at the ill-omened words. 'Oh no! The Brinsley Codd School for Sensible Thought is above all crash courses.'

'Pity!' said Mr Merryandrew with a melancholy sigh. He toyed listlessly with a piece of cold toast. 'And not very sensible, either. But send him there, anyway. Why not? Might as well!'

Anyone could tell he was in such an advanced state of car-despair, that he had totally lost interest in life, his own or anyone else's.

'I don't know if I want to go to a school for Sensible Thought,' Monty said rather nervously. 'I think I'm sensible enough already.'

'Take it from me, you need to attend that school immediately if not sooner,' Mrs Merryandrew said firmly. 'You may be a sensible boy in some ways, Monty, but no one who thinks he plays spaceships with ghosts is sensible enough.'

Chapter 4

A Typical Morning Scramble

'We'll call in on the principal of the Brinsley Codd School this very morning,' Mrs Merryandrew continued briskly. 'I'll telephone to make an appointment now. And while I'm at it, I'll also ring my coach, Mulgrew Twinge, and tell him to pick me up at the school – for the championship begins at quarter-past nine precisely, and I mustn't be a second late. It will mean a typical morning scramble, and just when I ought to be concentrating on the free-form section of the National Jigsaw Puzzle Championship. But I am prepared to scramble when my child's welfare demands it. I'll just warm up with a small jigsaw, and then we'll be off. And if I *should* win (which I might not do, what with worrying about my darling son, and our family car problems, not to mention the creative free-form section of the championship), the prize money will not only pay for a new car, but cover school fees as well. Now, tidy yourself up, Monty, and we'll be on our way.'

'Do I have to put on clean clothes?' Monty cried in dismay. He had already had one severe shock that morning, and the thought of having to dress all over again was more than he could bear.

Mrs Merryandrew glanced at the clock on the mantelpiece.

'Oh dear!' she exclaimed in rather a guilty voice.

'My time has been so taken up with jigsaw-puzzle practice that I haven't done the ironing. Just wash your knees. They look as if they've gone rusty.'

'That old car – the one Lulu and I play in – is extremely rusty,' cried Monty. 'The rust has worked right into me. I don't seem able to scrub it off.'

'Well, just paint your knees pink, then,' said Mrs Merryandrew. 'But don't be too long about it.'

She turned to Monty's father and laid a loving hand on his bowed shoulder.

'My dear,' she said gently. 'It is time to go to work, and you haven't had a mouthful of breakfast.'

'I'll take the red bicycle,' he said gloomily. 'You and Monty will need the tandem. How I wish I had concentrated on car maintenance at university instead of reading philosophy! I hope Monty learns from my mistakes.' He embraced her tenderly. 'I shall follow the progress of the championship on the radio, my darling,' he said. 'And if I should come up with a good idea for the creative free-form section, I will ring you at once. Don't worry about making any wholesome sandwiches for me. I'll grab a snack from the Krisp'n'Savoury man. You know! That fellow who sells fast food from a blue bicycle-rickshaw outside the Department of National Despair.'

Once Monty had painted his knees pink he looked extremely respectable. He and Mrs Merryandrew climbed on to the tandem.

'Brinsley Codd School for Sensible Thought. here we come!' cried Mrs Merryandrew. 'Pedal hard, Monty!'

The morning hasn't turned out quite as ordinary as I told Lulu it was going to be, thought Monty twenty minutes later as, both pedalling hard, he and his mother turned in at the great iron gates of the highly-respected school. It's been quite interesting so far. But I expect it will become boring any moment now.

Fortunately, he was entirely wrong.

Chapter 5

A Teacher to Worry About

Funnily enough, the principal of the school was actually called Principal . . . Ms Marigold Principal. All you had to do to remember her name was to remember her job, and all you had to do to remember her job was to remember her name. She had grey curls, and glasses, tinted blue. When Monty and his mother were shown into her office, she was bent over a thick pile of papers, whistling softly under her breath.

Monty supposed she was marking school exercises, and was amazed to see how happy she looked as she corrected industriously.

She must be a born teacher, he thought.

Ms Principal rolled her eyes and laughed to herself. Then she glanced up, saw Monty and his

mother in the doorway, turned bright red, and quickly slapped her lunch box on top of the school exercises.

'What can I do for you?' she asked, adjusting the lunch box so that nobody could accidentally read anything on the top page.

Mrs Merryandrew explained that Monty was having trouble with being sensible.

'There are times when being sensible is a problem for everyone,' said Ms Principal reassuringly. 'But the staff here work according to the teachings of Brinsley Codd, our founder. Look! There is his portrait. Doesn't he look like a sensible man?'

She pointed at a large painting which took up most of the wall behind her. It showed a thin-faced man with a wart on the end of his nose, and small, dark, piercing eyes.

'Atishoo!' Monty surprised both his mother and Ms Principal with the violence of his sneeze.

'Does the poor boy have a cold?' asked Ms Principal in a kind voice. All the same she took a step back, and placed a clenched fist firmly on her lunch box in case Monty accidentally blew it away with the power of his sneezes.

'He is allergic to dust,' said Mrs Merryandrew quickly.

'There is no dust in this school,' declared Ms Principal rather sharply.

'Oh no, of course not!' cried Mrs Merryandrew. 'But we may have opened the door too wide as we came in. A few specks could have floated in from the street outside. That's probably what happened, isn't it, Monty darling?' She gave his shoulder a little shake.

'Atishoo!' sneezed Monty, clapping a handkerchief to his nose, but staring over it at the picture of Brinsley Codd. Ghosts! he was thinking to himself. No doubt about it, the Brinsley Codd School for Sensible Thought is actually haunted.

At this moment there came a loud tooting from outside. It was Mrs Merryandrew's jigsaw-puzzle coach, Mulgrew Twinge, waiting to drive her to the championship. 'I'll be late!' cried Mrs Merryandrew. 'Do excuse me, Ms Principal. Oh, Monty, wish me luck!'

Between sneezes, Monty gave his mother a nimble kiss. Though he had to be speedy, he managed to be sincere as well. 'Atishoo!' he sneezed. 'Good luck! Atishoo!'

'Good luck to you, my darling boy,' she cried, cleverly avoiding the back-draught from his sneeze. 'Have a lovely day!'

'If I get a good idea for the creative free-form section of the jigsaw-puzzle competition, I'll ring and suggest it,' he shouted after her as she dashed to the door.

'Life is difficult for mothers who also have demanding careers,' said Ms Principal sympathetically. She and Monty watched Mulgrew gallantly hoisting the tandem into the back of his car (a flashy, red 'Snifitzu'). 'Now, Monty, if you come with me I will take you to your classroom and you can begin to settle down.'

But it is hard to settle down in a haunted school, no matter how sensible it appears to be in all other ways. And it came as no surprise to Monty to find, when Ms Principal led him to his new classroom, that the number on the door was thirteen – a most unlucky number. And when he clapped eyes on his new teacher, Mr Sogbucket, he knew at once that he was in deep trouble.

Chapter 6

The Quickest Turnaround in Educational History

As Monty stepped through the door of Room 13, an old dispatch case, locked with a big brass lock, immediately began rocking backwards and forwards, then toppled off Mr Sogbucket's desk and crashed to the floor. And not only this, but two children tumbled backwards off their chairs. Mr Sogbucket leaped to rescue his dispatch case, then swung on his heel to glare at the children.

So the ghost is following me around, thought Monty, but he knew it would be tactful to let Mr Sogbucket make the first comment.

'Calvin! Cora!' Mr Sogbucket cried, glaring at the children who had fallen over. He had cold, blue eyes, rather pointed yellowish teeth, and alarming black-and-grey eyebrows which came down so sharply when he frowned it was a wonder he managed to see anything at all from under them. 'Don't tilt yourselves backwards! I mean, is it sound – is it *sensible* to tilt yourself backwards? Is it *rational*? No! Backwards-tilting is totally forbidden at the Brinsley Codd School for Sensible Thought.'

'Please, Sir, I wasn't, Sir . . . I didn't, Sir! A mysterious force flung me right out of my chair,' cried Cora.

'Me, too!' said Calvin.

'There is nobody within reach of you,' said Mr Sogbucket. 'Don't make up such stories. Never forget that this is the Sensible School and we deal only in verifiable evidence . . . which means we only believe in things that everybody can see, hear, or smell. Now, did you children see, hear or smell anyone pushing Cora and Calvin off their chairs? Remember, I shall punish anyone who says they did.'

'No, Sir!' cried all the children in the room, shaking their heads.

'Atishoo!' Monty sneezed. His sneezes were growing more tempestuous. This time the sneeze was so violent it sent pencils and pens shooting right across the room to stick into the wall like darts.

Mr Sogbucket did his best to look kind and sympathetic, but it went against his true nature. He was a teacher of the old-fashioned, bitter kind, whose past life often seemed to him so much better than his present one. Many years ago he himself had been a pupil at the Brinsley Codd School, and he had had two glorious years as head prefect, making all the other children do exactly what he told them to do. But his time of glory was long past now, and though he didn't exactly want to be head prefect again, he certainly longed to be principal of the school he loved. However, the Board of Governors (all former pupils), were much too sensible to choose him.

'Do you have a cold, Monty?' he now asked in a sinister, silky voice, scrunching his eyes up as he spoke. The children shrank behind their books, trying to get out of range both of Mr Sogbucket's narrow gaze and Monty's sneezes.

'Ah! Ah! Ah . . .' gasped poor Monty.

'Did you say "Ha! Ha! Ha!"?' cried Mr Sogbucket. 'Are you *laughing* at me, Monty?'

'No, Sir!' gasped Monty. 'Ah! Ah! Ah . . . ATISHOOO!!!'

It was his biggest sneeze so far. Windows rattled. The door flew open, then slammed itself shut again. Drawings blew off the walls and flew around like birds; the free-standing blackboard slid off its easel; pieces of chalk ricocheted madly off walls and ceiling, somehow managing to scribble a few strange, jagged pictures before they dropped to the floor where they lay, trembling and chattering. The dispatch case wobbled wildly and would have fallen for the second time that morning if Mr Sogbucket had not clasped it to his heart.

'It is impossible to teach sensible thinking when someone is sneezing all the time,' he declared crossly. 'If Aristotle had sneezed as often as you,

Monty Merryandrew, he'd never have had a single sensible thought in all his life. Why do you do it?'

Monty could feel another sneeze rushing up through him.

'Ghosts!' he yelled, as it rose inside him like a great billowing blast. 'Some people are allergic to pollen, but I'm allergic to ghosts! This school has at least one ghost, and it is following me around. ATISHOO!'

The whole classroom shook as if battered by a hurricane.

'A ghost!' shouted Mr Sogbucket. What was left of his hair was standing on end. His silk tie was wrapped around his neck three times, and his glasses dangled from one ear. 'A ghost! I have a pupil in my class who believes in ghosts. Oh, the shame of it!'

On the tilted blackboard behind him a piece of chalk twitched. Then it began to draw. A remarkable picture took shape – a long-nosed face with tears running down its cheeks. It had a wart on its nose. Some children laughed, but Mr Sogbucket was furious.

'Right,' he cried, snatching up his dispatch case as he spoke. 'You don't impress me with your trickery. You have been in this class a mere seven minutes, but you are about to be expelled. That will be the quickest turnaround in educational history . . . another triumph for the Brinsley Codd School in its constant battle against sloppy thinking. Why, we might even get an entry in *The Guinness Book of Records*!'

A Ghost at Last

When Monty and Mr Sogbucket burst into her office together, Ms Marigold Principal was correcting school exercises once more. Hastily, she slapped her lunch box on top of them. Monty noticed that Mr Sogbucket was staring most suspiciously at the wad of papers under the lunch box, but he didn't have time to wonder why.

'Well, Sogbucket?' said Ms Principal, raising her powerful brows. 'You have come here for some sensible purpose, I take it?'

'Ms Principal,' said Sogbucket, tearing his gaze away from those papers. 'I'm sorry to say that this new boy has sneezed twenty-five times. He claims he is allergic to ghosts. I cannot be expected to teach under such difficult conditions.'

As he spoke, a curious thing happened. The painted figure of Brinsley Codd in the big portrait behind Ms Principal suddenly turned its head and looked keenly at Monty.

'This boy should be punished for his own good,' declared Sogbucket. 'I suggest that, during tennis practice, we hang him head downwards on that wall where the seniors drill themselves in forehand drives and power serving. That should make him think about something besides ghosts. And then, *after* tennis practice, I think he should be expelled.'

'That will do, Sogbucket!' said Ms Principal in a haughty voice. 'I am the principal of this school, not you.' At these words Sogbucket began grinding his teeth so fiercely that some of his fillings sent out little sparks.

'Now, stop it, Sogbucket. It is certainly not sensible to grind your teeth like that. And do you absolutely have to carry that old dispatch case with you everywhere you go?'

'Oh, believe me, I do,' said Sogbucket. 'There are deep personal secrets inside this case. Ha! Ha! Ha! I like to gloat . . . that is to say, I like to *ponder* over them from time to time.'

'Oh well, nothing wrong with a bit of pondering, I suppose,' said Ms Principal, trying to

seem good-natured. 'Now, off you go, Sogbucket. I will enquire into the sneezing incident myself.'

'Atishoo!' sneezed Monty, though, now that the portrait of Brinsley Codd was stretching and scratching its head and staring at him so intently, his sneezes had grown quieter and altogether more controllable. Indeed, as sneezes go, they were almost polite.

'But you will be too *kind* without me to remind

you of your duty,' whined Sogbucket. 'You will
ruin this boy with false mercy. Please let me
punish him – slightly. Please!'

'Back to the classroom, Sogbucket!' cried Ms
Principal, pointing imperiously to the door.

No one but Monty noticed the painted form of
Brinsley Codd rising to his feet. As Sogbucket
slunk away, carrying his dispatch case with him,
the painted figure looked around in a dazed

fashion. Monty's next sneeze was not much more than a sniffle.

'Now, about this obsessive sneezing, Monty . . .' Ms Principal began. 'Perhaps you need a little counselling? Shall we talk it through?'

'I'm allergic to ghosts,' Monty explained for the third time that morning – a morning which was certainly turning out much less ordinary than he had ever imagined it would be. 'As soon as I go into a place that's haunted, I sneeze. And I sneeze until the ghost actually shows itself. Then I stop.'

'Are you trying to tell me our school is haunted?' gasped Ms Principal.

'Yes,' said Monty, though he did not expect her to believe him. He stared boldly over her shoulder at the picture behind her. 'It is haunted by the ghost of a man with a long, thin face, scraggly hair, and a wart on his nose.'

'Brinsley Codd had a wart on his nose,' exclaimed Ms Principal. 'Are you suggesting that he is haunting his own school?'

'Well, I think he probably has a secret sorrow of some kind,' said Monty. 'Or a guilty secret. Or both.'

'Brinsley Codd guilty of something? Impossible!' exclaimed Ms Principal. 'It must be a secret sorrow.'

'It is both,' cried a strange, echoing, and not entirely sensible voice.

And the painted figure in the picture jumped right through his own gold frame like a circus dog jumping through a hoop. He landed lightly in a crouch on the floor, then straightened, touching his own arms and face as if he could hardly believe in himself.

'Oh, rapture, rapture!' cried Brinsley Codd. 'Visible at last. It's true. I do have a secret sorrow, and indeed I *do* have a guilty secret as well. And, at last, I can whisper them both into a well-washed and sympathetic ear.'

Chapter 8

A Secret Sorrow

'A secret sorrow?' gasped Ms Principal. 'Dear Mr Codd, do take care! A secret sorrow just doesn't sound sensible.'

'Not being sensible is part of my sorrow,' replied the ghost in curious, rushing tones, which swelled, died away, then swelled again like the sound of the sea. 'But we all have secrets, don't we? What about that great pile of paper, there, under your lunch box? What about that, eh?'

Ms Principal blushed a fiery scarlet. The ghost levelled a bony finger at her.

'You're not correcting a pile of school exercises, are you? Oh no!' he cried. 'You have been writing secret fairy tales, haven't you? You might as well confess. Hanging up there on the wall behind you,

I've been able to read over your shoulder quite easily.'

Ms Principal tossed her curls defiantly.

'I *like* fairy tales,' she said.

'Oh, I deeply sympathize,' said the ghost. 'I have enjoyed your stories. I would give you an 'A' grading if I were marking them. And, anyway, I myself, under the pretence of marking school exercises, once wrote a novel that was 800 pages long.'

'You wrote a novel?' cried Ms Principal. 'You! Was it ever published?' she asked, a faint note of jealousy creeping into her voice.

'No,' said the ghost. 'One day it just vanished . . . all 800 pages of it. And I was never able to open an inquiry, for there would have been a great scandal if it had ever come out that the principal of the School for Sensible Thought was actually writing racy novels when he was supposed to be marking school exercises. And while I was wondering where to look next, the school was struck by the Great Toasted-Cheese Fire of 1953. I'm afraid my 800 pages have gone for ever.'

'Is that your secret sorrow?' asked Monty inquisitively.

'No,' said Brinsley Codd. 'Well, it is secret, and it is a sorrow, but not the *main* sorrow. My *main*, secret sorrow is something much worse than that. You see, it was customary in those days for principals to be strict and stern. But I was secretly . . . I was secretly . . .' Here the ghost wavered, looking as if he might dissolve and perhaps drift back into the picture frame once more.

'Take a deep breath and concentrate,' said Ms Principal, speaking in a quiet, soothing voice.

'Ghosts don't breathe, Ms Principal,' Monty was forced to remind her.

'Oh dear, how tactless of me,' Ms Principal replied. 'Do forgive me, Mr Codd, and tell us your *main*, secret sorrow quickly – in case you fall to bits in some way. Are you worried about having been such a strict principal?'

'I was *supposed* to be strict and stern, but I never, ever managed it,' wailed the ghost in a miserable voice. 'In spite of all the clear thinking that went on in this school, certain children were occasionally naughty. Sogbucket was head prefect in those days, and he was always sending children to my office so that I could cane them. "Cure error through terror!" was something he used to say over and over again.'

'Sogbucket hasn't changed,' said Ms Principal with a sigh. 'But, rest assured, your canings have become legendary. Bad children used to come out of this office swearing . . .'

'Swearing?' cried the ghost, looking dismayed.

'Swearing to live better lives,' Ms Principal said quickly. 'You are in *The Guinness Book of Records* for caning.'

'That's just it,' moaned Brinsley Codd. 'I never ever caned anyone . . . not *one* pupil . . . not *once*. I couldn't cane a fly. I would talk to naughty children in a sympathetic but sensible way, and then I would. . . oh, the shame of it . . . I would tell them to *pretend* to cry, so that everyone would think they had been punished for their misdeeds. But then Sogbucket (did I mention that he was head prefect in those days?) listened at the study keyhole. He *said* he wanted to drink in my words of wisdom, but I know he was simply spying. Anyhow, he spoke to me bitterly, declaring that I had probably ruined the lives of all the children I had secretly refused to cane – and the lives of three extremely difficult pupils, in particular. Oh, I meant no harm, but now I cannot rest peacefully in my grave. Suppose Sogbucket was right? Suppose those poor, un-caned children went out in the world and lived jumbled-up, wicked, non-sensible lives, just because I didn't have the heart to punish them severely at the right moment.'

'I'm sure you don't have anything to worry about,' said Ms Principal firmly. '*I* don't take any notice of Sogbucket, and I never, ever cane anyone.'

'But you didn't live in the great, classical days of school caning the way I did,' sighed the ghost. 'The names of those three naughty children burn in my poor, tormented mind . . . Scrunley Filcher, Avery Crispins and Jessica Frogcutlet.'

'It would be hard to forget names like those,' agreed Monty.

'The first one, Scrunley Filcher, told terrible lies,' said Brinsley Codd. 'Avery Crispins thought nothing of poetry and art. All he cared about was making money . . . through cheating, if necessary. And the third one, Jessica Frogcutlet, absolutely refused to take an interest in embroidery or painting firescreens, or any other dainty, girlish pastime. Should I have caned them while I had the chance? Oh dear! Whatever happened to them, once they exploded into the world beyond school?'

'I expect they turned out reasonably well,' said Ms Principal. 'Most people do.'

'Help me! Help me!' wailed the ghost, wringing his hands so hard that his left hand came off and floated away on its own. Brinsley Codd grabbed it,

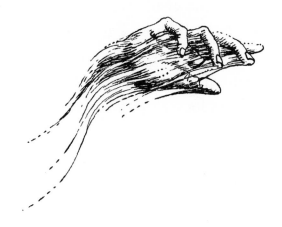

looking highly irritated, and pushed it back on his left wrist again.

'I'll help you,' offered Monty.

'How could *you* help?' asked Ms Principal, looking at him in surprise. 'I mean you live now, and all this happened *back then*. And all school records have been reduced to fine white ash by the Great Toasted-Cheese Fire of 1953.'

'Along with my 800-page novel,' mumbled the ghost of Brinsley Codd.

'I'll . . . I'll ask around,' said Monty. 'If I find out what has happened to them, Mr Codd's tormented mind will be at rest. And if we pretend it is a school project . . . an exercise, say, to punish me for unrestrained sneezing, Mr Sogbucket will have to stop nagging you.'

'Oh, what sensible thinking!' exclaimed Ms

Principal in a respectful voice. 'And what a lot of hard work.' She did not know that Monty was merely planning to run home and ask Lulu if she could remember anything about these long-ago children. 'How does Monty's plan strike *you*, Mr Codd?' she asked in courteous tones. But the ghost was vibrating in the way a rubber band vibrates after it has been used to fire a piece of paper right across the classroom. He began moaning.

'Oh, I'm going . . . going. I can't keep my shape any more. Remember me! While memory holds a seat in this distracted globe, remember me!' And he vanished back into the picture frame as if he had been sucked there by an invisible vacuum cleaner, where he struck a pose, more or less the same as the pose he had been holding when Monty first clapped eyes on him. Once again, he was nothing but a portrait.

'He certainly has a nice way of putting things,' said Ms Principal, looking at the portrait with admiration. 'What a scholar! And now we need to placate Mr Sogbucket.' She scribbled something on a piece of paper. 'Give him this, and tell him what hard work it is going to be,' she said, 'or he'll be back, grumbling and spying. I must confess, Monty (since you know so much already), that he is a difficult man. However, since he has been part

of the school
for such a long
time, I don't have
the heart to speak
sternly to him.
Now, off you go!'
    So off Monty went.

Chapter 9

A Kind-hearted
Rickshaw Man

It's all very strange, pondered Monty as he walked back from school that afternoon. This morning I looked ahead and thought it was going to be an ordinary, boring day. Yet bingo-bango! Here I am – suddenly enrolled at the School for Sensible Thought so that I'll stop believing in ghosts. But how am I ever going to stop believing in ghosts when the school itself turns out to be haunted? Oh well, I'll try and work it all out later, because right now I'm absolutely starving. What with the surprise of starting off at a new school, I didn't have much breakfast, and I forgot to pack any lunch. Actually, the whole day has turned out to be full of surprises.

As it turned out, the day had yet another

surprise in store for Monty . . . a nice one, this time.

A strange figure turned the corner ahead of him and came pedalling towards him in a blue bicycle-rickshaw.

'Krisp'n'Savoury Takeaways,' said the notice on the front of the bicycle. 'Fish bites, squidlets, sausosnacks, nipkin, and chips. Two free squirts of homemade tomato sauce with each serving.' But that was not all. The rickshaw, as well as the frame of the bicycle, was covered with words and pictures. Monty knew (for his father often

mentioned the Krisp'n'Savoury man with admiration) that the rickshaw was covered with art and poetry. Any poet who had not been able to get his or her poetry published was allowed to inscribe one poem on the Krisp'n'Savoury rickshaw. So people who bought a paperbag full of nipkin, or a sausosnack, had something to read while eating their lunch.

The little old Krisp'n'Savoury man was singing loudly to the music of his transistor, which dangled from the handlebars. A delicious smell accompanied him. As he reached Monty, he stopped singing and slowed down.

'Poor boy, you look so hungry!' he cried. 'And I – why, I've had a good day. One customer alone – a man from the Department of National Despair – bought almost all my stir-fry squidlets, golloped the lot, and then asked for chips as well. I think he must have forgotten to bring his lunch with him this morning. Anyhow, as it happens, I do have a few nourishing morsels left on my rickshaw hot-plate. Take them! Take them all!'

'Thank you, but I don't have any money,' said Monty doubtfully.

'Money!' cried the Krisp'n'Savoury man. 'Who needs money when they have the power of poetry and art, along with a bit of hard pedalling, to propel them through life? Well, I suppose we all do, really. Even *I* need a little bit, things being the way they are. But today I have made a fortune – enough to keep me going until tomorrow, or even the day after. It's true I have no squidlets left, but take this paper full of fishbites and chips. And here's some nipkin. I'm going home to make more. Eat this, and forget your troubles!'

And he thrust a sheet of newspaper, piled with crisp fishbites, chips, and several thin slices of cheesy nipkin, towards Monty.

Monty was quite happy to forget his troubles and other people's as well, yet as he seized the paper full of delicacies, he had the strange feeling that he had actually noticed something important, though he had no idea what it could possibly be. I've seen a clue of some kind, he thought, but what *was* it? However, before he could work anything out, he was distracted by a newsflash on the Krisp'n'Savoury man's transistor radio.

'In the latest action from the Jigsaw Puzzle Championship, Bella Merryandrew is surging ahead, having completed her first two sections in record time. Even the one-sided, thousand-piece puzzle, *Looking South into a Totally Cloudless Midday Sky*, was no problem to this amazing woman. But her coach, Mulgrew Twinge, is secretive

45

about her entry for the free-form section – the section in which she lost many points last year when she merely mixed five jigsaw puzzles and then fitted them together once more at an average rate of one piece every one-and-two-fifths seconds. Five mixed puzzles just do not have the creative mystery judges demand for a classic free-form presentation.'

Meanwhile, the Krisp'n'Savoury man had leaped on to his bicycle-rickshaw, and was pedalling on his way once more, smiling and whistling. Monty, too, went on his way, eating delicious fishbites, and feeling much refreshed. It was nice to have met someone so happy and kind on a day when everyone else seemed tormented with troubles of one sort or another.

What a day! he was thinking to himself. What next? Oh yes! Scrunley Filcher, Avery Crispins and Jessica Frogcutlet! They must all have been about the same age as Lulu. I do hope she can tell me what happened to them all.

Chapter 10

An Unusual Advertisement

When Monty wriggled around the last gorse bush in the corner of his garden he found Lulu sitting in the driver's seat of the rusting car, just as usual.

'You've been ages,' she cried impatiently. 'Come on! I can't play spaceships properly without you. You know all the right things to say like "blast-off" and "beam me down".'

'My mother decided to send me to the Brinsley Codd School for Sensible Thought,' Monty explained, 'and my father had to take my bicycle to work this morning, so it took me a while to walk home afterwards.'

'The Brinsley Codd School for Sensible Thought?' Lulu cried. 'I thought that school

would have fallen down ages ago.' There was a strange, scornful note in her voice that made Monty suddenly suspicious.

'Did *you* go to that school?' he asked sharply.

'Why do you want to know?' Lulu asked back.

'Because I've got to do a school project,' said Monty. 'And if you actually went to that school about seventy years ago you'll be able to help me. Just tell me – did you ever have anything to do with Scrunley Filcher, Avery Crispins or Jessica Frogcutlet?'

Lulu frowned as she struggled to pin down some highly slippery memories.

'That isn't a school project. It's just nosing into other people's business,' she replied at last.

'But that's what research is,' said Monty, and patiently explained that he was also doing secret work for the ghost of Brinsley Codd.

'Oh well, I don't mind helping another ghost,' Lulu said. 'Now, let me see. I certainly remember Avery Crispins . . . a really greedy boy with no interest in poetry, or car engines, or anything but money. And I *do* remember Scrunley Filcher,' she added. 'He wasn't greedy, but he was a great liar. If anyone said, "How are you today, Scrunley?", he would answer, "Very well, thank you, apart from the vampire bites", and then he'd make up a story which would curdle the blood. Some poor teachers had their blood permanently curdled by listening to Scrunley's excuses, and were forced into early retirement. I don't actually know what happened to either Scrunley or Avery, but I do know how we might find out.' She jerked her thumb towards the back of the car. 'Old newspapers have been blowing into this corner of your garden for the last forty years, and I've saved all those I could catch as they blew past. I expect Scrunley or Avery have made the headlines, probably for nasty business dealings or some sort of lying.'

Monty knew that the back of the car certainly was packed with hundreds of old newspapers.

'Let's get stuck into the research then,' said Monty. 'It's dirty work, but someone has to do it. Hey! We might even find a reference to Jessica Frogcutlet.'

'Whoever she was,' said Lulu discouragingly. 'What a name! She sounds like a dead loss to me.'

Monty and Lulu began by pulling the old newspapers from the bottom of the pile, and reading them carefully, searching for any mention of Scrunley Filcher, Avery Crispins or Jessica Frogcutlet. As they shuffled papers from one huge pile to another, they uncovered something in the back seat of the old car which Monty had never noticed before, for he usually sat in the front seat and took little notice of any car parts that might lie, rusting, behind him.

'What's this?' he asked, swinging a bracket out from a slot in one of the back doors. 'Hey! Is this a champagne glass sitting in it?'

'It's a vase,' Lulu said. 'There are vase-holders, complete with crystal vases, set in both the back doors of this car. My mother always had a single fresh crimson rose in each vase whenever we drove anywhere. Our chauffeur, Leopold, sat in the front seat, while my parents and I reclined in the back, drinking apple juice, eating little cakes, and sniffing the roses as we tooled through town. No wonder I loved this car. Not only did it have crystal vases, but its gear ratios were utterly sublime. Indeed, I may have loved this car a bit too much, which is why I'm stuck with haunting it now.'

Monty sighed as he picked up the next paper in the pile. He couldn't have cared less about the gear ratios but, for a moment, he thought rather wistfully of how lovely it would be to tool through town, sniffing roses and nibbling cakes. It would make such a change from eating breakfast while sitting on the floor each morning, before painting his rust-stained knees pink, and setting off for school on a red bicycle – *if he were lucky*. But then he saw something that drove all such thoughts right out of his mind.

'Look!' he cried triumphantly. 'It is! It really is! A piece about Scrunley Filcher.'

Lulu looked over his shoulder.

'An advertisement?' she exclaimed. 'Well, I suppose it's a beginning. What does it say?'

They read the advertisement together.

MOTORING GEMS
FROM SCRUNLEY FILCHER LTD . . .
PRE-LOVED CARS! RUST REVERSAL!
HONEST DEALING!

This was straightforward enough, but then the advertisement burst into poetry.

Scrunley Filcher's Good Advice
Is sound at thirty times the price.
We answer every motoring need.
Honest dealing guaranteed!
Rust fills others with dismay.
Scrunley whisks the rust away.
Please inspect our handsome yard –
Bowled-over-Backwards Boulevard!

'Bowled-over-Backwards Boulevard!' exclaimed Monty. 'And we're in Prang Street, so it's just around the corner. Let's go!'

Lulu looked a little melancholy.

'It's all very well for you to say "Let's go!"' she sighed. 'I'd love to say "Let's go!" myself. But I have to haunt this particular car, remember, and this particular car is never going anywhere ever again.'

'But you can get *out* of the car,' Monty said. 'I've seen you walk around it.'

'Only as long as I keep one hand on it,' said Lulu. 'The minute I take both hands off . . . Fzzzzt! I get sucked back inside again. It's one of the rules of haunting.'

Monty suddenly had a brilliant idea.

'But what about those vases?' he suggested. 'They're part of the car. Would the rules of haunting allow you to haunt one of the vases for an hour or two? If so, I could carry you with me.'

A look of joy passed over Lulu's pale face.

'It just might work,' she cried. 'Oh, Monty, you're already far too clever for the silly old School for Sensible Thought. They should make you head prefect straight off . . . or even principal. Let's try!'

Monty held out one of the crystal vases in front of him, and Lulu did something that only ghosts can do. She dissolved. One moment she was there, looking almost real, and in the next she had disintegrated into a lot of coloured specks, all spinning and dancing around one another like a cloud of bright midges. The coloured specks whirled around for a second, then flowed down into the crystal vase. Peering inside, Monty saw Lulu sitting on the bottom of the vase, looking surprisingly at home there.

'Off we go!' he called down to her. His voice echoed strangely, as if the crystal vase were much bigger inside than it was outside. Lulu clapped her hands over her ears.

'Off we go,' Monty repeated, whispering this time. And off they went, around the Prang Street corner, across Impact Drive, and into Bowled-over-Backwards Boulevard, a handsome street, filled with small factories and a large number of used-car yards.

Chapter 11

Truth in a Used-car Yard

The used-car yards of Bowled-over-Backwards Boulevard were particularly festive, for most of them were strung with little coloured flags, flicking and flapping in the city breeze. Monty noticed that the used cars all displayed large notices, printed in capital letters, saying what wonderful bargains the cars were. AMAZING VALUE, said one notice. EXCELLENT CONDITION, VERY CHEAP! ALMOST FREE! said another. ONE PREVIOUS OWNER (A MAN OF THE CHURCH), said a third.

Monty wandered along the boulevard, looking for Scrunley Filcher and making a note of any good bargains which he could tell his father about later that evening. Music, and occasional commentary on the Jigsaw Puzzle Championship poured from various sound-systems on either side of the street. Bella Merryandrew was apparently into the double-sided section, and absolutely racing through it. There was even a rumour she had broken her own record, working at a rate of a piece successfully placed every one and one-fifth of a second.

Suddenly, Monty stopped.

'What's happened?' called Lulu.

Monty did not reply at once. He was staring into a small yard filled with a few particularly battered cars. There was nothing unusual in that, of course. It was the notices on the cars that had brought him to a standstill. 'TOTAL JUNK!' said the notice on the nearest windscreen. 'TERRIBLE BRAKES!' screamed another. 'NOT WORTH THE PRICE!' admitted a third. Among these battered cars and honest notices sat an old man in a blue overall, carefully spraying some mysterious substance on to a piece of rusty tin.

And then Monty saw the notice set high over the gate of the car yard.

SCRUNLEY FILCHER – USED CARS
SKILLED RESTORATION
RUST PREVENTION
UNNATURALLY HONEST DEALING

Lulu gave a small but scornful laugh.

'Scrunley Filcher! Honest dealing! Not very likely!' she cried.

'But look at those notices. They do seem honest – almost too honest,' said Monty. 'He can't sell many cars.'

He walked up to the old man.

'Please! Could you tell me if you are Scrunley Filcher?' he asked politely.

'No,' said the old man, concentrating on his piece of rusty tin. 'My name is Neroli-Pompas.'

'Well, I can't help noticing that you've got the
name Scrunley Filcher over your gate – and
embroidered on your overalls, too,' said Monty
rather sternly.

The old man looked up with a sheepish smile.

'Oh, all right! I admit it,' he said with a sigh. 'I
am Scrunley Filcher. I like to tell a lie every now
and then, as long as it's totally harmless, just to
keep my hand in. But I always tell the absolute,
utter truth about my cars. It's not easy – indeed it
is against nature – but I do it.'

'You can't make a lot of money telling the truth about used cars,' Monty said. 'Not if you tell the *whole* truth.'

Scrunley Filcher looked grave.

'I lose money,' he admitted, 'but it doesn't matter too much. My real business is restoring fine old cars to their former glory. I love to show off, so let me show you this!'

He leaped with surprising agility to a nearby garage door and flung it open. A magnificent car was revealed. It was dark green and gold, with big wheels, wide running boards, and a hood that folded back so that fresh air could flow over both driver and passenger.

'Now, this is a 1908 Triumph-Podmore,' said Scrunley Filcher, letting his fingers trail caressingly over its nearest mudguard. 'It is in perfect condition, thanks to my restoration techniques which include the use of my secret *Revorust* process, and I shall sell this car for a lot of money – when I can bear to part with it, that is. So I can afford to tell the truth about my used cars (which I must do because of a secret, sacred childhood vow), and still feel fairly cheerful about the disadvantages. Are you looking for a used car yourself?'

'I was looking for you,' said Monty. 'I believe

you were once a pupil at the Brinsley Codd School for Sensible Thought.'

'So I was,' agreed Scrunley Filcher.

'Wonderful!' cried Monty. 'I've already found one of them, and it's only four o'clock.'

'One of who?' asked Scrunley, looking around him, rather anxiously.

'I am here on behalf of a ghost,' said Monty. 'The ghost of Brinsley Codd. He's been fretting over certain pupils, wanting to find out what happened to them after they left school. *You* are one of the pupils he remembers best.'

'And I remember him! Never will I forget Brinsley Codd – that noble man,' Scrunley cried excitedly. '*Saint* Brinsley, I sometimes call him (just to myself, you know). And you say you are in touch with his ghost? But perhaps you are lying, though I would be the first to forgive you if you were.'

'No! I'm able to see ghosts,' Monty explained, 'and only this morning I saw Brinsley Codd.'

'Oh, then take me to him this minute,' cried Scrunley. 'Worrying about me, is he? I want to put his poor old mind at rest, and I want to do it in person.'

'I don't know,' said Monty a little doubtfully. 'The school might be all locked up by now.'

'We'll set off at once in the Triumph-Podmore,' said Scrunley eagerly, 'and I'll pick the lock of the school door if necessary, for I never took any secret, sacred childhood vow where lock-picking was concerned. It'll be a bit of an adventure, and in a Triumph-Podmore, too.'

Monty began to feel jittery. Suppose they broke into the school, and then Brinsley Codd was unable to materialize? However, he felt he had to take the risk. Folding his fingers carefully around the crystal vase in his coat pocket, Monty climbed into the passenger seat of the Triumph-Podmore. And within a very few minutes they were tooling along in fine style, while pedestrians (and even other drivers, if safety permitted), burst into spontaneous applause at the sight of the wonderful old car, so perfectly restored.

As they came towards the city centre they passed the Krisp'n'Savoury man who had stopped by the roadside to paint a new poem on the side of his rickshaw.

Try one chip and you'll want twenty!
Don't hesitate, for I have plenty.
Criminals convert from knavery
For morsels cooked by Krisp'n'Savoury.

He waved to them cheerfully as they overtook him. And a moment later, gliding past the front door of the Department of National Despair, Monty actually glimpsed his own father. His nose was flattened against a first-floor window, and he was staring so longingly at the beautiful Triumph-Podmore that he utterly failed to notice Monty, his own son, sitting in glory beside the driver.

Chapter 12

Furtive Scuttling

For the second time that day Monty found himself climbing the wide, marble steps that led into the Brinsley Codd School. The door was not only unlocked but wide open, so he led the way through corridors which echoed strangely, now that all the children had gone home.

'How it all comes back to me!' murmured Scrunley Filcher, gazing in rapture at large photographs of past pupils which lined the walls (all looking keen and sensible).

But before they reached Ms Principal's haunted office, they ran into none other than Mr Sogbucket, scuttling along in a curious, *furtive* way – not the sort of sensible scuttling one would expect of an ex-prefect. Sogbucket did not see them at once, for he was looking guiltily over his shoulder as he scuttled, clutching his black dispatch case. Running right into Scrunley Filcher, he sprang back in his tracks with a hoarse cry, rather like a man who thinks he may have collided with a maddened gorilla. Nevertheless, he recovered quickly.

'This school is closed,' he cried in a bossy voice. 'Come back tomorrow.'

'I've been doing my research project, Mr Sogbucket,' said Monty. 'I have found Scrunley Filcher.'

'Sogbucket? Can that be you?' exclaimed Scrunley. He turned to Monty. 'Sogbucket used to be the wickedest head prefect ever to change gear on one of the sharp corners of life, and do you know, he hated all romance and fairy tales. Look! He's shuddering at the mere mention of them.'

'Any sensible thinker shudders at the mention of fairy tales,' cried Sogbucket.

'What nonsense, Sogbucket!' cried a new voice. Ms Principal had come briskly out of a left-hand corridor, and now stood frowning at them. 'Fairy tales transcend the boundaries of mere conscious self, Sogbucket.'

'You *would* say that,' said Sogbucket. 'Fairy stories are lies, and that's all there is to it.'

But Ms Principal's eye had fallen on Monty.

'Monty Merryandrew!' she cried. 'How nice to see that you are already so fond of your new school that you cannot tear yourself away!'

'Remember that project you set me?' said Monty. 'Well, I have found Scrunley Filcher, and I have brought him here to testify before . . . you know who,' he whispered, looking anxiously at Sogbucket whose ears seemed to be bending forward, eager to catch every private word.

'That ghost? He's probably haunting my office at this exact moment,' said Ms Principal, not in the least worried about mentioning ghosts in front of Sogbucket. 'Do come and speak to him, dear Mr Filcher. I'd like to have this haunting business cleared up once and for all.'

'What's this?' cried Sogbucket. 'A principal of the School for Sensible Thought who not only defends fairy tales, but believes in *ghosts*? I shall inform the Board of Governors immediately.'

'I have sensible reasons for believing in the ghost of Brinsley Codd,' retorted Ms Principal. 'Just come with us, Sogbucket, and see for yourself.'

Sogbucket, who was boiling with indignation, suddenly looked furtive once more.

'I'd love to, but I can't. I have so much work

waiting for me at home,' he whined. 'I have a whole pile of school exercises to mark.'

But Ms Principal grabbed his arm with a principal's special grip, friendly yet sufficiently firm to cut off all circulation to the fingers. He just *had* to go where she was taking him . . . straight towards the haunted study. Monty, carrying his crystal vase with Lulu inside, followed them, while Scrunley Filcher, clutching the keys of the Triumph-Podmore, came last of all. Ms Principal swung the door of her office wide. There was a moment of silence. Then everyone gasped in horror.

Chapter 13

Confetti and Gillygaloos

The room seemed to be entirely filled with tiny scraps of paper. Scraps of paper lay like a fall of snow over the floor. The breeze, caused by the opening door, lifted other scraps in a slow fountain so that stepping into the room was like entering an Antarctic blizzard. Ms Principal stared around her room as if she expected a sledge, and men in bulky snow suits, to appear out of the cloud. Then she snatched one of the pieces of paper out of the air in front of her, squinted at it, and let out a piteous cry.

'Look!' she cried. 'The word "gillygaloo"! Now, I must be the only person in the city to have used the word "gillygaloo" over the last few weeks.'

Scrunley Filcher, Monty and Lulu looked at

one another blankly. Monty felt he should at least show an interest.

'What *is* a gillygaloo?' he asked.

'It's a bird remarkable for laying square eggs,' said Ms Principal. 'People don't mention them very often. But can't you see what this means? It means that the ghost has torn my fairy tales into mere confetti. He must have been jealous of my stories because his own novel vanished during the Great Toasted-Cheese Fire of 1953. Well, if I lay my hands on him he'll wish he was even more of a ghost than he is now. He'll wish he were a mere *ghost* of a ghost.'

'But where *is* this ghost?' asked Scrunley Filcher.

'Yes, where *is* it?' cried Sogbucket, laughing in a wicked, though somehow uneasy, fashion.

'If I get my hands on him, he'll learn something about being sensible he did not know before,' mumbled Ms Principal. And, as she glared around in a way that would have made any ghost think twice, Monty began sneezing.

'Ah! Ah! Ah! *Ker-choo!*' he cried, while scraps of fairy stories whirled about him.

'Don't breathe in!' screamed Ms Principal. 'You might swallow some vital word. Oh dear, it was my only copy, too.'

Monty sneezed again.

'Brinsley Codd must be close at hand,' he cried. 'Everyone concentrate. Help him to take shape!'

'What rubbish!' muttered Sogbucket. 'Brinsley Codd is dead and gone. Anyhow, he wasn't as great as people make out. Any school teacher who spends valuable exercise-marking time writing an 800-page novel is only pretending to be sensible.'

Yet, there before their very eyes, the snowstorm of whirling paper began to take shape . . . the shape of Brinsley Codd himself. Suddenly, he was among them, staring angrily at Ms Principal.

'Is this a rational way to run an office?' he shouted. 'Look at it! When I was in charge here, all waste paper was strictly confined to the waste paper basket. But these days the basket is completely empty because all the paper is flying through the air.'

'Waste paper!' yelled Ms Principal. 'In a really well-run office there is no such thing as waste paper. These scraps whirling in the air aren't *waste paper*. They are the remains of a fine book of

fairy tales – the very ones you saw me writing this morning. You were jealous, weren't you, Mr Codd? Just because you'd stupidly mislaid your own 800-page novel you were jealous of my fairy stories, and so you tore my manuscript into little bits.'

'Never!' cried Brinsley Codd in a hooting, haunting voice. 'I would never – no, never – tear another writer's book into confetti.'

'Well, who did, then?' asked Ms Principal. 'That book certainly did not tear itself up.'

But Brinsley Codd's eyes, keen as pins even though they were so ghostly, had fallen on Scrunley Filcher.

'Oh,' he cried. 'Can it be? Is that you? Is it really little Scrunley? But how you've aged!' he added in amazement.

'Of course I've aged,' snapped Scrunley Filcher. 'That famous occasion – the one when you didn't cane me – was about seventy years ago.'

'Are you sure that your habit of telling lies hasn't caused you to crumble away before your time?' asked Brinsley Codd suspiciously.

'I promise you I haven't told a single lie for years,' Scrunley said with profound sincerity. 'Well, none that matters! Just a few harmless ones, such as pretending my name is Neroli-Pompas.

This lad here said you feared I might have gone to rack and ruin because of not being caned, so I set out at once in my Triumph-Podmore to put your tortured mind at rest.' He shot a quick glance round the room and, seeing that he had the attention of everyone except Ms Principal (who was still desperately snatching pieces of paper out of the air), he launched into his story, speaking rather quickly so he could get it over and done with before people grew sick of it. And, as he spoke, the remains of Ms Principal's fairy tales slowly drifted through the air around him.

Chapter 14

Scrunley's Tale

'I remember the occasion so well. Sogbucket sent me to your room to be caned for . . . for improving the truth a little. I was utterly terrified, for your canings were notorious. I went to your room, trembling both inside and out! My teeth were chattering. All I had to do to knock on your door was lay one knuckle against it. My trembling took care of the actual knocking. You looked out, frowning thunderously. Your hand fell on my shoulder, and you snatched me inside.

'But behold! Once the door – that very door over there – closed behind us, you changed. It was like summer sun coming out from behind black and threatening clouds. You smiled. You forgave me. You told me you understood. Lying was the

75

basis of all great literature, you told me, though of course we must struggle to grow past the magic of the lie and attain the deep truth that lies beyond. Your simple words went to my childish heart. I staggered out of your room pretending to cry (which is what you told me to do) so that people would think I had been caned.

'I remember getting as far as the school steps, and pausing in a patch of sunlight. Suddenly, it was just as if I had emerged into a brighter, more perfect world. The trees, the grass, even the bike-shed seemed to sparkle with a magical dew of

forgiveness. Why, it was as if I had never seen the sky before. What pure and perfect blueness! In that moment I knew then, even though honesty would destroy the family business of selling second-hand cars, I would never tell a lie again.

'But I had to work out some other way of making a living. Right then and there I began to invent *Revorust*, the revolutionary rust-reversal process which has made my fortune. Mr Codd, I owe everything to you and your sublime act of kindness. I thank you!'

Scrunley struck a fine, dramatic attitude, and there was a round of applause from all those present, all except for Sogbucket who looked from one to the other in utter bafflement.

A beatific smile crossed the features of Brinsley Codd.

'Oh, thank you, thank you!' he cried. 'If Jessica Frogcutlet and Avery Crispins have turned out equally well, I'll be able to give up being a ghost and flow on to whatever comes next.'

'None of this is any help to me,' grumbled Ms Principal, sighing so deeply she nearly swallowed a few scraps of her own precious confetti. 'My valuable manuscript has been ripped to shreds. And if Brinsley Codd didn't do it in a fit of mad jealousy, well, who did?'

'And what about the others? Dear little Avery? Or Jessica Frogcutlet?' asked Brinsley Codd, ignoring Ms Principal and turning to Monty. Everyone in the room could see hope shining in his ghostly eyes.

'Alas,' said Scrunley Filcher. 'Jessica died young.'

Brinsley Codd gave a wavering cry.

'What? Little Jessica struck down in the flower of her youth?' He looked critically at Scrunley Filcher. 'Still, it is better than lingering on. How you must envy her!' Then his expression changed. 'Oh! Perhaps she came to some tragic end simply because I did not cane her when I had the opportunity. Perhaps it was because I let her walk away without challenging her irresponsible ideas. You know, that girl wanted to be a motor mechanic? Can you imagine it? A girl who refused to take an interest in embroidery! A girl who wanted to spend all her time talking casually about universal joints and big ends? Of course, *I* blame her parents. I well remember how they used to drive through town, reclining in the back seat of their elegant car, supping apple juice, eating little cakes, and sniffing at red roses. Now, that's not a sensible sort of life, is it?'

Monty's jaw dropped. His gaze swivelled

downwards. Lulu was looking up at him with an apprehensive expression. She glanced away quickly.

'You know, there is something very strange about this,' said Ms Principal, who had not been concentrating in the way a principal ought to concentrate when ghosts are under discussion. 'If Brinsley – oh, I do hope you don't mind me calling you by your first name, Mr Codd?'

'Be my guest!' said the ghost gloomily.

'Well, if Brinsley did not tear my pages of fairy stories to pieces, then who did? Because somebody must have. And whoever did it must have spent quite a lot of time over his wicked work. Tearing

500 pages of A4 paper into confetti takes time, as well as desperate strength.'

'Well, I must be going,' cried Sogbucket, pretending to look at his digital watch. 'I don't have time to spend on this sort of thing. Torn-up fairy tales! Ghosts! It's disgusting. It will ruin the school's reputation.'

He made a dash for the door, but Ms Principal caught his arm in her famous, special grip.

'You're forgetting your dispatch case,' she said, rather ominously.

'Is that the same case he used to have when he was a prefect?' cried Scrunley Filcher, snatching it up before Sogbucket could reach it. 'I remember how he used to prance around with this very case then.'

'Give me that case!' shouted Sogbucket. 'It contains important documents.'

'I always wanted to look inside it,' cried Scrunley Filcher, 'and now I'm going to. I'll bet he was just showing off about nothing all the time.'

'Give it to me!' yelled Sogbucket, and for a moment the two ancient men wrestled with the case, just as if they were boys at school again. The dispatch case was old and battered and could not stand such wild treatment. Its brass catch gave way. As it burst open, a second huge, billowing cloud of confetti . . . yellowish confetti, rose from it. For a moment it was impossible to see from one side of the study to the other.

Chapter 15

The Gongoozler Clue

'What did I tell you? He's been carrying rubbish around with him,' cried Scrunley Filcher scornfully, from the centre of the dense, yellowish cloud. 'I've told so many lies myself I can recognize a lie a mile off, and I always knew Sogbucket was lying when he went on about how important his papers were. I mean, look at this piece here . . .' He was peering down at the small piece of paper clinging to the back of his hand. 'I see the word "gongoozler" here. "Gongoozler"! Utter nonsense.'

'Hang on a moment!' protested Brinsley Codd. 'Everyone knows that a "gongoozler" is someone who stares for hours at anything out of the ordinary. Now, I used to get a lot of gongoozlers in my classes when I was a teacher, so naturally the hero of my novel (my 800-page novel that vanished into nothing, that is) was something of a gongoozler himself. I commented on it every ten pages.'

Suddenly, the air sizzled, and the crystal vase in Monty's hand jiggled wildly. Coloured specks surged out of it into the room. Lulu stood before them.

She trembled. It seemed she might collapse back to nothing, but then she snatched the crystal vase from Monty, and, sustained by contact with part of the old car, she kept her shape.

'You dummies!' she cried scornfully, while Brinsley Codd stared at her with amazement verging on awe.

'Jessica!' he shouted. 'It is she! Jessica Frog-cutlet.' He looked at Monty. 'Why didn't you tell me you had brought Jessica with you?'

Chapter 16

Gloating Over the Gallynipper

M onty looked at Lulu.

'Why didn't you *tell* me?' he asked wearily.

'But I *like* the name Lulu,' said Lulu, 'and I grew totally sick of the name Frogcutlet. My father kept telling me I had to live up to it. But forget the Frogcutlet side of things! Don't you realize what's been going on? All these *new* scraps of paper are really *old* scraps of paper. It's Mr Codd's missing novel. It wasn't destroyed in the Great Toasted-Cheese Fire of 1953, because someone had already torn it up. Someone had already *stolen* it. And someone has been carrying it around all that time, secretly *gloating* over it. And it absolutely, utterly has to be someone who hates stories!'

Brinsley Codd squinted at a scrap of paper as it wavered down towards the floor.

'You're right!' he cried in great excitement. 'Look! There goes a word I used in my novel . . . "gallynipper" . . . a large mosquito, that is. I know! I know! Any writer might use a word like that, but there – *there* – floating next to it is a much more difficult word – "gyascutus". I can certainly remember when I used *that* particular word. Mine was a challenging book.'

'What *is* a gyascutus?' asked Monty curiously.

Brinsley Codd shrugged carelessly, though anyone could see he was longing to show off his knowledge as all teachers, and even the ghosts of teachers, love to do.

'A gyascutus is a huge four-legged animal, with its legs longer on one side than on the other,' he explained learnedly. 'This means it can walk about on steep hillsides with particular ease, though always in the one direction, of course.'

'Is it herbivorous?' asked Ms Principal, doing her best to show off herself.

'Stop showing off!' cried Lulu. 'Don't you realize? There is someone in this school who tears up other people's books because they make him think of the mystery of life and it frightens him. All new thoughts sting him like gallynippers.

They frighten him, too.
Work it out! Be sensible!
I challenge you all!'

There was a second
during which
everyone in the
room did their
best to think
sensibly. Then
all eyes swivelled
towards one
person. Every voice
in the room, except
one, spoke a single
name.

'Sogbucket!'

Chapter 17

Sogbucket Snuffles

Sogbucket glared back at them all. Then he burst into wicked laughter.

'All right! I admit it,' he yelled. 'Why not? I am the sensible one who should have been in charge of this school. One of *my* sensible thoughts is ten times . . . a hundred times . . . as sensible as anyone else's. Brinsley Codd? Well, what about Brinsley Codd? He locked himself away in his room writing a novel . . . a *novel*, mind you! Something invented! Made up! Mere fancy! And Ms Principal is even worse. Fairy tales, indeed!'

'But you used to write stories yourself,' cried Lulu, pointing at him. 'I remember distinctly! When you were a prefect you used to try writing stories about vampires.'

'Did he?' cried Brinsley Codd. 'I never knew that.'

'He used to *begin* those stories, but he could never *finish* them,' Lulu said. 'I expect that is what has made him so jealous and bitter.'

Sogbucket glared around him, but Lulu's thought was so sensible that he couldn't argue with it. Instead, he burst into tears.

'Oh, very well,' he wept, snuffling into a handkerchief which was not only clean but starched as well. 'I admit it. I was jealous of anybody who wrote books – and actually managed to *finish* them. I used to sneak in here after dark and read Brinsley Codd's novel. "Ha! Ha! He'll never finish it!" I thought to myself, laughing with bitter joy. But he *did* finish it,' cried Sogbucket, thumping the desk with his fist. 'Horrakapotchkin! I just couldn't stand it. So – yes – I stole his novel, and tore it to pieces. I thought I'd discourage all teachers at the School for Sensible Thought from making up such stories. But then, years later, I found, through creative snooping, that Ms Principal was writing fairy tales. *Fairy tales!* Well, there they are, all bobbing in the air around us. Ah, ha ha ha ha ha!'

'I wouldn't laugh just yet,' said Monty, for an amazing idea had occurred to him. 'Will the Triumph-Podmore hold us all?' he asked Scrunley Filcher.

'Easily,' Scrunley replied. 'Those cars were built in the days when people had big families.'

'Does anyone know where the school vacuum cleaner is kept?' asked Monty. 'We must vacuum up every single precious piece of paper at once.'

'I don't know that we need bother with the

vacuum cleaner,' said Brinsley Codd. 'We ghosts are a sort of vacuum in ourselves. Perhaps if little Jessica and I . . .'

'Don't call me "little"!' cried Lulu. 'And don't call me "Jessica"! Still, he's right! We do have a few mysterious powers. Hold that dispatch case open.'

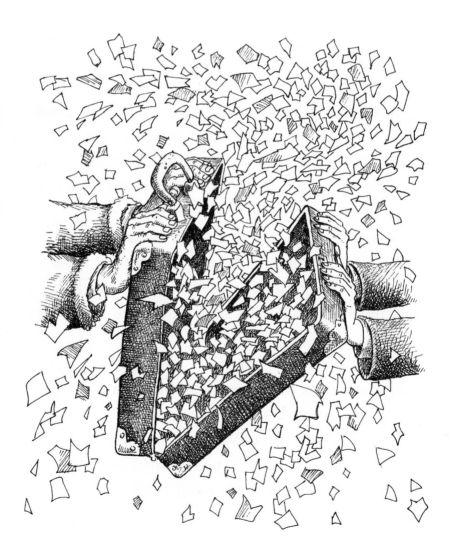

'Shutting it will be the real trouble,' said Scrunley Filcher, holding the case with its broken brass clasp as wide open as possible. Both Brinsley Codd and Lulu shut their eyes and seemed to concentrate hard.

At first nothing happened. Then something like a small whirlpool formed directly over the dispatch case, and the scraps of paper began to funnel down into it. It was as if that dispatch case were starving for confetti. Within a few minutes every scrap of paper, white and yellow, every gongoozler and gallynipper, was crammed into the case. Scrunley Filcher slammed it shut. Its sides bulged dangerously. Ms Principal quickly snapped several huge rubber bands around it, and sealed it with sticky tape.

'You fools! You'll never put those pages together again,' shrieked Sogbucket.

'Don't be too sure!' shouted Monty. 'I have a plan, and, not only that, I have a remarkable mother. Bring that big roll of sticky tape and follow me!'

And to his delight, everyone, even Sogbucket, *did* follow him as he barged out of the office, carrying Lulu (who had quickly climbed back into the crystal vase), down the marble steps, and into the waiting Triumph-Podmore.

Chapter 18

A Scrap of Rust

Scrunley Filcher turned out to be a particularly careful driver – almost too careful.

'Faster! Faster!' cried Monty, as they approached the last set of traffic lights before the Jigsaw Puzzle Championship car park.

'No way!' said Scrunley Filcher. 'I am not running the risk of denting my Triumph-Podmore. And, of course,' he added quickly, 'I don't want to squash any little child who might stagger out into the street due to inadequate parenting.'

The lights turned red. Scrunley Filcher slammed on the brakes of the Triumph-Podmore.

Monty howled with despair for about thirty seconds . . . quite a long time for a despairing howl. He was sure he had the key to his mother's success, and also to the happiness of Brinsley Codd and Ms Principal, and yet it was taking him ages to reach his mother's side. Filled with anguish, he clenched his left hand into a fist and thumped his own knee so fiercely that flakes of rust showered out from under the pink paint, even shooting as far as the driver's seat. Scrunley Filcher idly picked up one of the rust flakes and, frowning, thought he recognized it from somewhere.

'Funny!' he said. 'This fragment of rust reminds me of . . .'

But then the light turned green.

'Quickly!' said Monty, but Scrunley Filcher had

already placed the flake of rust carefully on top of the instrument panel and had spun the Triumph-Podmore through a smart left-hand turn into the championship car park.

There was a huge crowd outside the gate eagerly watching every detail of the Jigsaw Puzzle Championship on gigantic television screens. A famous former champion was commenting on the style and speed of the competitors.

'And there's no doubt that, once again, Bella Merryandrew is the star of the occasion. She has shown that she can do big patches of sky without the slightest hesitation, even in the double-sided jigsaw section. She has simply ripped her way through the jigsaw of Hermann von Plomp's great medical painting, *Cleopatra with Chicken-pox*, as if she found it easy to tell one pock from the pock next to it. But Isleworth Eastwick has done very well, too, and he has already declared himself for the Innovation Free-Form section. He says he will reassemble an entire computer from microscopic, electronic relays. Whereas Bella Merryandrew is still keeping *her* free-form project a secret. In fact, we hear she may fall back on five mixed, thousand-piece, two-sided puzzles – that's five thousand pieces in all. It might even count as ten thousand pieces since each piece has two sides.

Technically difficult, of course, but I don't think five mixed, thousand-piece, two-side puzzles would score a single point for originality.'

Holding Lulu in her crystal vase, Monty led Scrunley Filcher and Ms Principal (who was carrying the ghost of Brinsley Codd, tucked in with the mixed fragments of the two fine books, in Sogbucket's dispatch case) towards the main concourse. Sogbucket, snickering sarcastically, followed them. They all went into the championship stadium which was criss-crossed with many long tables. Jigsaw-puzzle enthusiasts crouched over these tables, staring in despair at the jumbled pieces spread in front of them. As Monty walked on, a competitor suddenly leaped up, screaming and clawing at the table in front of her. Trained St John's Ambulance volunteers, accompanied by a psychiatrist and a counsellor, closed in rapidly, but Monty swept by. He could see his mother in the distance, her fingers twinkling effortlessly. Mulgrew Twinge paced up and down beside her.

'Mum!' yelled Monty. 'Mum!'

Mulgrew Twinge leaped in front of Mrs Merryandrew, holding out his arms to prevent Monty from rushing to his mother's side.

'How can you be so selfish?' he cried. 'She needs to concentrate. Right this moment, Bella Merryandrew is more than a mere mother.' But when Monty explained he had an original project that might be of use to his mother in the free-form part of the championships, even Mulgrew looked thoughtful. At that moment Mrs Merryandrew slotted the last piece of the advanced section into place. Television cameras zoomed in, and an official hurried over.

'Mrs Merryandrew!' he cried. 'Congratulations! I don't want to put pressure on you, but you must now declare exactly what puzzle you are planning to do for the free-form section. We need to know in the next ten seconds.'

Monty leaped in beside his mother and grabbed the microphone.

'She is going to do something so challenging that it will stand as a monument of skill in jigsaw-puzzle circles for many years to come,' he shouted. His distraught mother swung round, looking both startled and hopeful.

'I have brought the puzzle, just as you asked me to,' Monty said, giving her a secret nudge and a wink. 'In this dispatch case . . .' (he rapped the top of the dispatch case as Ms Principal staggered up with it) '. . . we have the ghost of a repentant headmaster, and the typescripts of two large books, one 800 pages long, the other a mere 500. These books have both been torn into scraps, not one of which is bigger than a thumbnail, and many of which are mere confetti. Mrs Merryandrew will not only separate the two books from one another, but will put them together again, page by page. A team, highly trained in sensible thinking, will pass her small pieces of sticky tape but apart from that she will work entirely without assistance.'

'Oh Monty,' cried his mother, clasping her hands in an attitude of prayer. 'How right I was to send you to the Brinsley Codd School for Sensible Thought. It's paying off already.'

She turned to the official. 'Have you written that down?' she asked him sternly.

'I'll just rush the announcement to the judging panel,' the official said. 'If I hurry, I should get there with at least three seconds to spare.'

Sogbucket, spiteful to the last, tried to trip him up, but the official was used to jealous and resentful jigsaw-puzzle specialists and leaped over his extended foot with graceful ease.

'She'll never do it,' said Sogbucket, though he did not look quite as sure of himself as he had seemed to be a moment earlier.

'You silly man,' said Mrs Merryandrew, picking up a scrap of paper from the box. 'I'll do it easily. "Gyascutus"!' she read aloud. 'Well, you don't see many of them these days, do you?'

'Do you *know* what a gyascutus is?' asked Monty incredulously.

'Of course I do,' his mother said. 'It's an animal with legs that are longer on one side than on the other. Everyone knows that.'

And at that exact moment Scrunley Filcher gave a great cry.

'I have it!' he yelled. Monty looked over at him. During the discussion of the free-form section, he had taken a jeweller's glass from one of his pockets, and had been frowning over some strange microscopic fragment that intrigued him. Now, Monty realized it was the same flake of rust that had flown from his knee when he thumped it in despair, back at the traffic lights.

'Do you know what this is?' cried Scrunley, tenderly holding the flake of rust, and gazing at it as if it were a pearl of rare price. 'The structure of this rust shows me beyond all doubt that it originally came from a true Neroli-Pompas. There is no doubt about it. The car of my wildest dreams is rusting away somewhere in this very city. Where is it? Who can take me there? For, judging from this rust, there is not a moment to spare. I'll trade anything you like to mention for a genuine Neroli-Pompas, particularly a model from the classical days of the 1920s.'

For the second time that day Monty had a moment of inspiration.

'Would you trade a Triumph-Podmore?' he asked slyly.

'A Triumph-Podmore! What's a Triumph-Podmore?' yelled Scrunley scornfully. 'Pooh to the Triumph-Podmore! I can find five or six of them in this country alone. Give me a Neroli-Pompas, and anyone who wants it can drive my Triumph-Podmore away with him.'

'But suppose the Neroli-Pompas is a particularly rusty one?' Monty asked him cautiously.

'Rust!' cried Scrunley Filcher. 'Who mentions rust to the inventor of *Revorust?* I thrive on challenges. Just lead me to this poor, neglected classic of a car, and I will bring about an act of car restoration that will take your breath away.'

Lulu looked out of the crystal vase.

'Do you mind *haunted* cars?' she asked.

'They're all haunted,' said Scrunley. 'Don't try to frighten me, Jessica Frogcutlet.'

'Well, put it like this . . . would you be prepared to give lessons in car maintenance to a ghost?' Lulu asked. 'Even if that ghost happens to be the ghost of a girl?'

'Any girl who haunts a car must be serious about car maintenance,' replied Scrunley. 'I wouldn't have the slightest hesitation.'

Monty looked over at his mother. She was well into the free-form section. Huge television screens showed her fingers twinkling as they separated the yellowish, old paper from the white. At her elbow, Chapter One of Brinsley Codd's novel was rapidly being reassembled. Mulgrew Twinge had whipped out his mobile phone and was talking to a publisher on the other side of town. 'And what about film rights?' Monty heard him saying. 'After all, these books have been saved from almost certain destruction. There has to be an angle in *that*!'

Ms Principal was passing little strips of sticky

tape to Brinsley Codd who was placing them
exactly where Mrs Merryandrew told him to place
them. For some reason his ghostly fingers were
extremely nimble with sticky tape. But this might
have been because sticky tape is transparent and a
little ghostly itself.

Then, who should come shouldering his way
through the crowd but Mr Merryandrew, pushing
Monty's red bike in front of him. How worn and

tired he appeared . . . a real tribute to the
Department of National Despair.

Monty longed to shout words of encouragement
to him, but he did not dare to break his mother's
concentration. Carrying Lulu in the crystal vase,
he raced to his father's side. Scrunley Filcher
followed him eagerly.

'Dad, I've good news for you!' Monty hissed.
'It's just what you've been waiting to hear.'

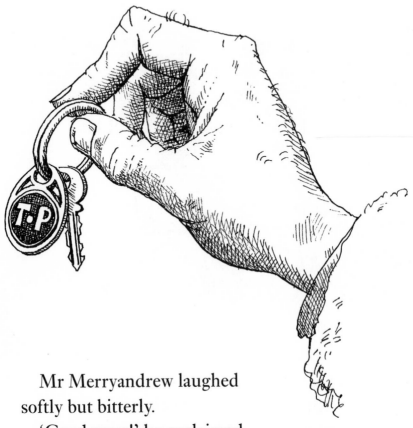

Mr Merryandrew laughed
softly but bitterly.

'Good news!' he exclaimed.
'There's no such thing as good news any more.'

'There is! There is!' insisted Monty. 'Mum's
going to win the championship. And this is
Scrunley Filcher, an honest used-car salesman –
the very man you've been longing to meet, who is
also longing to meet you. If that isn't good news, I
don't know what is!'

Scrunley Filcher took one look at Mr Merryandrew, and fell on his knees, his arms spread wide.

'Can you – can you possibly be – the owner of a rusty Neroli-Pompas?' he cried. 'And, if so, will you trade it for a fully restored Triumph-Podmore?'

'Well, I . . .' Mr Merryandrew hesitated and looked at Monty in confusion.

'Say "Yes!"' hissed Monty.

'I'll throw in an extra 500,' cried Scrunley. 'That Neroli-Pompas must be mine, even if it *is* haunted by Jessica Frogcutlet.'

'Say, "Done!" Dad,' Monty hissed again. 'Trust me! It's the chance of a lifetime.'

'Done!' exclaimed Mr Merryandrew.

'Oh joy! Oh joy!' exclaimed Scrunley. 'Here are the Triumph-Podmore keys. We must not wait a moment longer. Lead me to the poor, rusting ruin so that I can begin the restoration process at once.'

But Mr Merryandrew, overcome by excitement, shock and happiness, and a long day's work in a government department, had fainted clean away.

Chapter 19

A Rusty-car Party

'I thought you said it was going to be an ordinary, boring day,' said Lulu a little later. She was sitting on the rusty bonnet of the Neroli-Pompas (which had been tenderly hauled through the gorse and into the middle of the meadow that passed for a lawn at the Merryandrew house).

'OK! So I made a mistake,' said Monty, who was sitting beside her. 'I must have been getting mixed up with tomorrow.'

All around them a great party was in progress. Scrunley Filcher was going over the fine old car with a magnifying glass, laughing with delight as he uncovered details of beautiful if crumbling craftsmanship. Beyond him, Mr and Mrs Merryandrew, sitting side by side in the Triumph-

Podmore, toasted each other with glasses of jigjag fizz, a wholesome drink much loved by jigsaw-puzzle champions. Mulgrew Twinge was pouring out further firkins of jigjag fizz for the runners-up in the National Jigsaw Puzzle Championship. He was talking over his shoulder to a group of publishers who had been thumbing through the pages of two fine books, now restored to almost perfect condition by the clever, flickering fingers of Mrs Merryandrew, jigsaw puzzle champion, and many strips of sticky tape applied by Brinsley Codd and Ms Principal. A huge, silver cup sat between Monty and Lulu on the bonnet of the Neroli-Pompas . . . the cup for the National Jigsaw Puzzle Championship.

Sogbucket stood, holding his glass of jigjag fizz, frowning in bafflement as the publishers praised the 800-page novel and the book of fairy tales, and outbid each other for the right to publish them.

'What sort of reward do I get for years of trying to live a sensible life?' he cried in despair. 'I have struggled to be sensible myself. I have struggled to teach sensible ideas to others. But where has it got me?'

'Well, you can't complain . . . not really,' said Ms Principal. 'I mean, here you are supping jigjag fizz. And you don't really deserve it, Sogbucket,

you know you don't. However, forgiveness is so utterly sensible that I forgive you freely. Indeed, if you promise to read my fairy tales, one every night, I will dedicate the book to you.'

'To me?' cried Sogbucket. Tears sprang to his eyes and to hide his emotion he took a large, spluttering mouthful of jigjag fizz. 'A book dedicated to me?'

Mr Merryandrew stood up in the Triumph-Podmore.

'We need food!' he shouted. 'I'll just run inside and make toast for everyone.'

'Oh, my dear,' said Mrs Merryandrew. 'Let's live dangerously. Ring the Krisp'n'Savoury man and ask him to bring unlimited squidlets, fishbites, chips and nipkin.'

Mulgrew Twinge overheard this.

'I'll ring him on my mobile phone!' he shouted.

Monty smiled at the happy scene.

'I suppose you'll have to go and live in Bowled-over-Backwards Boulevard,' he said to Lulu. 'I'll really miss you, not to mention our spaceship games.'

'It's not very far to Bowled-over-Backwards Boulevard,' she pointed out. 'You'll be able to visit me whenever you want to. And, I must say, haunting will be a lot more interesting if I get a few lessons in car maintenance, not to mention a chance to go tooling around town in our old style.'

'Well, it will take a while to restore this car,' Scrunley Filcher said. 'But, with the aid of

Revorust, I am sure I will have it in sparkling condition by Christmas. And then we'll certainly all go for a spin, with holly as well as red roses in the crystal vases. Oh, what a day of joy this has turned out to be. And we still have so much to look forward to.'

'I never, ever dreamed . . . not even in my wildest dreams (which were pretty wild),' murmured Mr Merryandrew, 'that I would one day be the owner of a Triumph-Podmore. A real, actual, genuine Triumph-Podmore in mint condition! Who would ever have thought it?'

'Who would ever have thought that I would win full marks in the free-form section of the National Jigsaw Puzzle Championship?' Mrs Merryandrew sighed, glancing rapturously at her big silver cup.

'Whoever would have dreamed that my book would be published?' declared Brinsley Codd, looking almost entirely real with the excitement of the moment. 'Especially after the Great Toasted-Cheese Fire of 1953.'

'I always thought my book of fairy tales would collect dust and cobwebs in the bottom drawer of my desk,' said Ms Principal. 'Do you know, I think I shall give up being a principal and write another book while I'm still in the mood.'

A flicker of hope shone in Sogbucket's eyes.

'If I reformed . . .' he said craftily. 'If I forced myself to admit that even the most sensible things have – well – a trace of mystery in their hearts – perhaps I might hope to be principal my-self some day.'

'We'll see,' said Ms Principal, giving him a suspicious look. But then she relaxed and smiled. 'Yet, who knows?' she added. 'If you promise never ever to tear other people's stories to pieces again . . . no matter how jealous you may happen to be . . .'

'I never will,' exclaimed Sogbucket eagerly. 'In fact I might try to find one of my old vampire stories and have a go at finishing it.'

'Likewise you must promise never, ever to think of caning a pupil again,' added Brinsley Codd.

'I have become a better and deeper man in the last hour,' Sogbucket declared fervently.

But at this moment the Krisp'n'Savoury man arrived on his blue bicycle-rickshaw, and people forgot jigsaw puzzles, cars, books and schools for (apart from the two ghosts), they were all as hungry as hunters, and the squidlets and nipkin smelt simply wonderful.

'You know,' said Lulu, narrowing her eyes as she stared across at the little old Krisp'n'Savoury man giving out goodies right and left, 'I have the strangest feeling that I've met that man before. But I couldn't have met him, could I, Monty? Hey! Monty!' she exclaimed, for Monty himself was staring at the Krisp'n'Savoury man in utter amazement.

'I've just realized something,' he said. 'Krisp'n'Savoury! Avery Crispins! The Krisp'n'Savoury man is the third pupil of the three that Brinsley Codd was so worried about. He's the cheater! The one who was mad on money! Yet only today Krisp'n'Savoury gave me a whole free paper bag of fishbites and chips. What on earth can have happened to him?'

Chapter 20

A Krisp'n'Savoury Life

'He can't be,' said Lulu. 'Avery Crispins was totally different. And yet . . . you know, Monty, you just might be right again.'

At that moment Brinsley Codd himself let out a shrill and ghostly cry. He was staring in amazement at the little old man sitting in his bicycle-rickshaw, passing out paper bags full of delicious food.

'Avery! Little Avery!' he said. 'Oh, what has life done to you?'

'Mr Codd, can it be you?' cried Avery Crispins – for it was, indeed, he. 'Oh, how often I have wanted to fall on my knees before you and offer grateful thanks. I know I was a greedy boy in the past, Mr Codd. I know I was obsessed with mere cash-in-hand. But never will I forget that fatal day when Sogbucket sent me to your room so that you could cane me for a slight case of cheating other more stupid – that is to say, more *trusting* – pupils out of their lunch money. I went into that room with all my savings in my pocket, planning to bribe you to let me go, for in those days I thought money could achieve everything. And then, before I could so much as draw my loaded money-box from my pocket, you smiled at me. You offered me a drink of lemonade and a plate of cheese biscuits, and talked to me in such a clear, kind and sensible way. Mr Codd, I saw . . . I suddenly saw . . . that a generous heart, reinforced with a few good recipes, was worth far, far more than anything else in the world. How often I have thought of you as I fried my squidlets in pure vegetable oil . . . how often have I longed to thank you in person! And I *will* thank you.'

He turned to the assembled jigsaw puzzle people, family members, ghosts, car enthusiasts, and principals – past, present and possibly future of the School for Sensible Thought. 'I will only charge for fishbites and chips,' he announced loudly. 'Every squidlet, every sausosnack and every slice of nipkin will be free from this moment on.'

So the party went on, with lots of eating, and licking of sauce from fingers, and lots of laughing and singing, until late into the night. Neighbours gave up trying to watch television and joined in. More and more people crowded in at the gate to join the fun, to admire the two fine old cars, and exclaim over the great silver jigsaw-puzzle cup.

'What an unexpected day it has been,' said Monty to Lulu. 'And only this morning I thought it was going to be boring.'

'But every day has the chance of surprises in it,' said Lulu. 'I mean I might think tomorrow will be exciting, and yet it might turn out to be totally boring and ordinary. You never can tell.'

'Well,' said Monty, looking around at the celebrating people dancing light-heartedly in the meadow grass that passed as a lawn at the Merryandrew house, 'perhaps it's best not knowing for sure how any day is going to turn out. Some days begin happily and end in trouble. Other days begin in trouble, and end with a party.'

'I like the second sort best,' said Lulu. 'But you're right, Monty. And it's the hidden surprise of things that keeps life interesting . . . even for a ghost.'

'Or even for a boy,' said Monty. And as he said this, it suddenly seemed that surprises were lurking in the heart of everything, and that even a sensible life could be unexpectedly full of ghosts, jokes, old cars, stories, puzzles, and astonishment – and that that was the best way for any sensible life to be.